MEET THE AUTHOR - ANTHONY MASTERS

What is your favourite animal?
My bantams
What is your favourite boy's name?
David
What is your favourite girl's name?
Penny
What is your favourite food?
Chinese food
What is your favourite music?
Mexican
What is your favourite hobby?
Canoeing

MEET THE ILLUSTRATOR - HARRIET BUCKLEY

What is your favourite animal?
A cat
What is your favourite boy's name?
Ernest
What is your favourite girl's name?
Emily
What is your favourite food?
Spinach
What is your favourite music?
'There She Goes' by The La's
What is your favourite hobby?
Playing the harmonica

To Robina who brings light
With much love and thanks

COMHAIRLE CHONTAE ÁTHA CLIATH THEAS
SOUTH DUBLIN COUNTY LIBRARIES

MOBILE LIBRARIES
TO RENEW ANY ITEM TEL: 459 7834

Items should be returned on or before the last date below. Fines, as displayed in the Library, will be charged on overdue items.

You do not need to read this page – just get on with the book!

First published in 2002 in Great Britain by
Barrington Stoke Ltd, Sandeman House, Trunk's Close,
55 High Street, Edinburgh EH1 1SR
www.barringtonstoke.co.uk

Reprinted 2005

This edition based on *Tod in Biker City*, published by Barrington Stoke in 1998

ISBN 1-842990-55-1

Printed in Great Britain by Bell & Bain Ltd

Contents

Chapter 1
Waiting for Dad

"When will Dad be back?" asked Tod.

"He'll be here soon," his mum told him.

Tod gazed out of the window and down to the beach with its piles of rotting weed and white fish bones. There was no life here because it hadn't rained for a very long time. The sea was far away now.

"Tod, Dad won't come back just because you want him to!" his mum went on.

Tod Hunter was 13. His dad had a gift that others did not have. He could find water under the ground. He had a stick which he held in his hand and it moved by itself when water was near.

There was very little water anywhere and many people had died already.

There was panic. People would do anything to get hold of water. It was not safe to live in the cities, so Tod and his family went to live by the sea.

Tod lived with his mum and dad in a house near the beach. Years ago, lots of people used to visit. Now, no-one came.

There was miles of sand. Near the road, the trees were black and dead. There was no green to be seen, because there was no fresh water.

"I'm scared that the Bikers may have got Dad," said Tod. "They've been looking for someone to find water for them."

"Don't get in a state about it. Your dad can look after himself," said his mum.

But Tod knew she was scared too.

"I'm going to take the buggy out and look for him," said Tod.

He needed a drink badly. It was always like this. He and his mum had to share out the little water that they had. Tod drove his beach buggy over the sand hills to the road. Then he heard the sound of an engine. It wasn't Dad's jeep. It was a bike.

Tod came to a stop behind a rock, just as a Biker came round the corner. The bike was large, black and shiny.

The Biker was dressed in black and he had a skull and crossbones painted on his helmet.

The Biker stopped and looked in his bag for his bottle of water. He took a long drink.

Tod saw him stretch out his arms and yawn. Then he turned round and drove back the way he had come.

I hope he doesn't meet Dad, thought Tod. The Bikers were outside the law. They went around in gangs. They robbed people and beat them up to get their water.

Tod waited until he could no longer hear the sound of the engine. Then he drove home in his buggy. As he drove back, Tod looked up at the grey sky. He gave a shiver in spite of the heat.

Chapter 2
A Scorcher

"I think that awful hot, dry wind we get these days is coming back," said Mum, when Tod got home. "We'd better go down to the basement and take some more food with us."

Tod hated this wind. It was so hot that it was called a Scorcher.

"And Dad's not back," said Tod sadly. It was no fun for Dad to be out when that awful hot, dry wind swept in from the sea.

"I expect something's kept him," said his mum.

Tod made up his mind not to tell her that he'd seen a Biker. It would make her more scared than ever.

Tod did not sleep much that night. Had the Bikers got his dad? Was his dad being made to find water for them?

When Tod did sleep he could hear his dad in his dreams. "Help me, Tod! You've got to help me," he was saying. In his dream Tod tried to run to his dad. But his feet sank into the sand.

When at last he woke, he ran into his mum's room. Dad had not come back.

"Where is he?"

"Not here yet." She was looking out of the window. "That awful wind's coming now."

Tod gazed at the steel grey sky. These winds were so hot and dry that they could burn away human flesh.

"I've put all we need in the basement," said his mum. "Let's get down there. Dad will be OK."

Tod and his mum sat in the basement and looked at the sand spilling through the cracks in the wall. "He'll have found somewhere to shelter from the wind," his mum went on.

If the Bikers haven't got him, thought Tod to himself. But out loud he said to his mum, "He'll be home soon."

Soon the sound of the wind was so loud that they could hardly hear themselves speak. It was very hot in the basement. Mum told Tod to drink some water from the jar on the floor.

"Go on, Mum," said Tod. "You have some water too." But she shook her head.

The wind blew itself out at last and was silent. They went upstairs. The house was OK, but there were piles of red-hot sand against the door. Then Tod heard a roar.

"That can't be the wind coming back," began Mum.

Tod knew what it was. He could see the Bikers riding towards the house across the sand hills.

Chapter 3
Unwanted Visitors

"Quick, get out the back door, Mum. The Bikers are on their way. We can hide in the wood," yelled Tod.

"Why are they coming *here*?" asked his mum.

"To see if they can find any maps or papers to show them where there's still water," replied Tod.

"Dad keeps them in the safe," said Mum.

"They could blow it open," Tod told her.

They looked at each other.

"The Bikers must have got Dad," said Tod's mum, "or why are they coming here?"

"We have no time to talk. Let's go," Tod replied.

Tod and his mum ran outside and into a wood of bare, black trees.

They ducked down as they heard the Bikers coming closer to the house. Then the Bikers stopped and switched off their engines. There was no sound for a long time.

"What's going on?" asked Mum.

"I can't see," said Tod.

Then they both heard the sound of a door being kicked in. They waited for ages. Something was being dragged out of the house. There was a soft thump.

"That's the safe," said Tod in a low voice.

There was another long wait. Then they heard a loud bang.

"That *was* the safe. They've blown it up."

Had the Bikers hurt Dad? Had they tried to make him talk? And had they come to the house because he would not tell them anything?

The engines revved up again.

"One of them may have stayed behind as a look-out," said Tod. "I'm going to creep over to the house. You stay here. We don't want them to get both of us."

Tod went slowly up to the house in case there was still anyone there. The door had been broken down, and the safe lay open on the sand.

Now Tod was very angry. What right had the Bikers to walk into his home like this? And what had they done to his dad?

"I told you to wait in the wood," he said to his mum as she came up to the house.

"Don't you tell me what to do." She was very angry. "Just look at all this mess! I'm fed up with it. We must go and find your father."

"*We*?" Tod asked.

"Yes. You go north and I'll go south," his mum told him. "He could be anywhere."

"Biker City?"

"Could be," she said.

"Then I'm going south," Tod told her. "I've got the buggy. That's faster than your old car."

"Take care," she begged.

"We've *got* to find him, Mum."

"What can we do against the Bikers? It's hopeless," said his mum.

Chapter 4
Tod Alone

When they got to the main road, Tod went one way and his mum went the other. They had filled their bags with as much food and water as they could carry.

"Don't take any silly risks, will you?" said his mum.

"It's all a risk now, Mum. You know that."

21

Mum began to cry. "I know," she said. "God be with you."

Tod's mum hadn't said that to him for years. Not since their old home had been burnt down by the hot wind. They had had to find somewhere else to live.

Tod's mum waved to him until she was out of sight.

He revved up his buggy and sped off over the sand hills.

Then he saw a dark shape. As he got closer, Tod saw that it was a water tower. A skull and crossbones was painted on the side in red. Tod knew he would be mad to drive any closer. He would have to hide the buggy in the sand hills and walk.

In front of him the sun was blazing down on a heap of rusty old lorries, buses, cars and railway trucks.

Tod hid behind a pile of rocks. Where had the Bikers gone? He thought he heard something move behind him. A few metres away, there was a pile of old oil drums. Had the noise come from there?

He couldn't see anything, because the sun was too bright. He turned back and gazed at the scrapyard where the Bikers lived. Where were they? And, most important of all, what had they done with Dad?

Then something large and solid landed on Tod. It pushed him down into the hot sand. Tod rolled over, and kicked out. The stranger fell over on his back. Tod jumped to his feet and threw himself on top of the boy, who was dressed in the black gear of the Bikers. Tod landed with his knees on the boy's chest and held down his arms. The boy tried to shake him off, but Tod was too strong for him.

"Where are the Bikers?" Tod asked.

"Don't know," the boy told him.

Tod pressed down with his knees and the boy howled with pain.

"Where *are* they?"

"Don't know," said the boy again.

"You've got to tell me."

"I won't."

Tod had a quick think. The boy was looking scared. Did he think Tod was going to kill him?

"Do you want some water?" Tod asked.

"You got some?" The boy's lips were dry.

"Two bottles," Tod told him.

"As much as that?" said the boy.

"What's your name?"

"Billy." He looked up at Tod. He did not trust him. "How do I know you've got water?"

"You'll have to trust me." He pulled a bottle of water out of his bag. "I'll swap you half of this."

"What for?" asked Billy.

"You've got to tell me where they've taken my dad."

Billy looked at the water. He licked his lips. He was longing for a drink.

"Give me the water first," he said.

"No way." Tod shook the bottle and the water sloshed around inside. "Not till

you've told me where they've taken Dad and how to get there."

Billy gave in. "They're down at the old tin mine. It's on the other side of the city. They found your dad there looking for water. He thought he was safe because we were away on a raid."

"Why did they go off without you?"

"I nicked some water from the tower. Not much. Just a few drops, but they were mad with me. So they left me behind. You go right through Biker City. There's a sign to the old tin mine. Now where's that water?"

Tod gave him the bottle. Billy drank as if he would never stop. "That's all you get," said Tod.

But Billy went on drinking. Tod grabbed the bottle from him.

"One thing," Billy said.

"What's that?" asked Tod.

"Don't grass me up. They'll kill me."

Tod went back to the buggy and drove off through Biker City. He looked back at Billy. He looked so lonely that Tod felt sorry for him. But he had to find the old tin mine. He had to find Dad.

Chapter 5
A Cry in the Dark

A hot wind from the sea blew the sand into Tod's eyes. They began to sting badly. Then at the very end of Biker City, he saw a sign which said TIN MINE.

Tod drove on. He came to a pile of broken down cars which gave him some cover. It was very, very hot. Tod was scared that the Bikers might come back at any moment.

Tod looked ahead. There was silence everywhere. Just a few gulls were flying over the bare fields.

Slowly he drove on. Then he saw the shabby, old tin mine. There were lots of motorbikes parked outside, so Tod drove the buggy back the way he had come, trying not to make any noise.

When he got to the pile of smashed cars, he hid the buggy behind them. Then Tod jumped out onto the sand and ran back to the mine again. He checked to see if the beach buggy could be seen. Yes, a small bit of the buggy stuck out from behind the cars.

Then he saw the Bikers coming out of the mine. Tod hid himself in a ditch under a pile of sand. All the time he was scared that the Bikers would see the bit of the buggy that stuck out of the pile of cars. If they *did* see it, they would come and look for him.

Tod lay flat in the ditch as the Bikers drove past at speed. The dust from the bikes choked him. When he lifted his head, Tod saw them riding away, bent low over their bikes.

The Bikers had been going too fast to see the buggy. Phew, that had been close. Tod got to his feet. He went back behind the pile of cars and hid the buggy better.

Then Tod began to walk slowly back to the tin mine. He looked out for danger all the time.

When he got to the mine, there seemed to be no-one around. But the silence scared him. His heart thumped. Tod got to the open mineshaft and looked down into the dark hole. What was he going to do?

Tod lay down and stuck his head into the black shaft. The Bikers might creep up on him at any moment.

In spite of the fact that he had not seen Billy coming, he had been able to deal with him.

But he was much stronger than Billy. Tod knew he would be no match against a real Biker.

"Dad?" he yelled. "Are you down there? Can you hear me, Dad?"

Silence. Maybe his dad wasn't down there after all.

Tod tried again. "Dad," he yelled. "Can you hear me?"

Then he heard a shout from far down below.

Tod yelled down the shaft again. This time he was sure he heard his dad's voice.

"Dad! Hang on. I'm coming down."

Tod knew the old tin mines were not very deep. By good luck there was a ladder there too. He could still hear someone shouting down in the shaft but he couldn't hear what he was saying.

Tod didn't wait any longer. He stood up, and grabbed the top of the ladder. Down he went into the dark.

Chapter 6
Descent into Darkness

Tod began to feel more and more safe as he went down. He was going faster and faster when he came to a sudden stop. He had got to the end of the ladder. There was just a black hole under him.

If only Tod had got a torch with him. It was dark all round him and there was only a bit of light from the top of the shaft.

He looked down and felt scared. Then the dim light of a torch shone up at him. He had found Dad at last.

"They've chopped off the bottom of the ladder, so I can't get out," Dad told him.

"I'll jump," Tod called down to him.

"Go back! Please, Tod," said Dad. "There's no way you can help me."

"You know I'd never leave you down there."

"You'll only get trapped yourself as well. Go back home. I'll sort this out," said Dad.

"I'm coming down, Dad. I'm going to jump."

"Wait!" Dad told him. "Let me move over so I can catch you."

Tod looked down. What if he broke a leg? They would both be trapped down there in the dark.

But what could he do? He *had* to jump.

"Are you ready?" asked Dad.

"I'm coming. Now."

Tod let go of the ladder. The fall seemed to take a long, long time. Then he felt a thump as he landed on Dad. They both fell on to the ground.

Tod was lying on top of Dad and Dad had his arms around him and was hugging him. Tod got to his feet. He was OK. Nothing was broken. He picked up the torch and shone it on Dad who was finding it hard to stand up.

"You OK, Dad?"

"You knocked the wind out of me," his dad panted.

"How did you get here?" asked Tod.

"I was looking for water and the Bikers found me. They said I had to work for them, but I said no," Dad told him.

Tod could see that his dad's face had marks all over it.

"They beat you up!"

"I wasn't going to give in. I said I wouldn't work for them. So they cut off the last part of the ladder so I couldn't get out. They've gone now, but they said they'd come back tomorrow as soon as it was light."

"What are they going to do then?" asked Tod. He was scared.

"They said I was to think things over. If I won't find water for them, they'll kill me."

"But you haven't found any yet."

"That's the problem. I *have* found water," said Dad.

Chapter 7
A Dangerous Discovery

There wasn't much light coming from the torch now. Dad set off down a tunnel and Tod went after him. Then Dad stopped and picked up the stick which he used to find water. When he pointed it at the wall, the stick began to twist and turn.

"That means there's water on the other side," said Dad.

"How do we get at it?" asked Tod.

"I've got two hammers with me. The rock's thin and cracked here. If you and I work very hard we might be able to smash a hole through to the other side."

"Aren't you glad I found you?" said Tod.

"Your mum will be very upset by now. She won't know where you are."

"She'll still be out looking for *you*," Tod told him.

He's a brave lad - I've just got to save him

Tod could see the tears in Dad's eyes. "Let's get to work then," Dad said.

They hammered away at the rock for over an hour.

"I'm sure I can smell water," Dad said at last.

But Tod could only smell the dampness of the tunnel. The hole they had made in the rock seemed very small. He felt worn out. They began to hammer away again. The torch had gone out a long time ago, but Tod had a watch on him which lit up after dark.

"It's the middle of the night. How much longer are we going to keep on with this?" asked Tod.

"We've got to work faster. The Bikers will be back as soon as it gets light," Dad told him.

Chapter 8
Swim for your Life!

After two more hours of hard work, a large chunk of rock fell inwards. There was a splash.

"We made it," said Dad. We can both get through this hole in the rock wall now."

He was right. Tod felt much better now.

As Dad began to creep through the hole in the rock into the dark on the other side, they both heard a noise far back in the tunnel.

"You said they wouldn't come till it got light, Dad," hissed Tod.

"They must need a drink badly," Dad replied.

The water came up to their knees in the dark space behind the rock wall. Then a beam of light cut into the dark.

"Stop!" yelled a Biker.

"There's water in there. We can drink," Tod heard one of them say.

"Keep going," Tod told Dad. "We've got to go where the water goes."

But the water was getting deep. It was up to their waists. Then Tod hit his head on something.

"The tunnel ends here," he said. It was a shock.

"No, the tunnel hasn't ended," Dad told him. "It's just that the water goes under the ground here."

More torchbeams lit up the tunnel. By their light Tod and Dad could see that the water went under a ledge of rock.

"This is the end of us," said Tod in a low voice.

"The water may come out into a cave." Dad was more hopeful.

"Let's dive," said Tod. "The Bikers don't need you now. They'll kill us both if we go back."

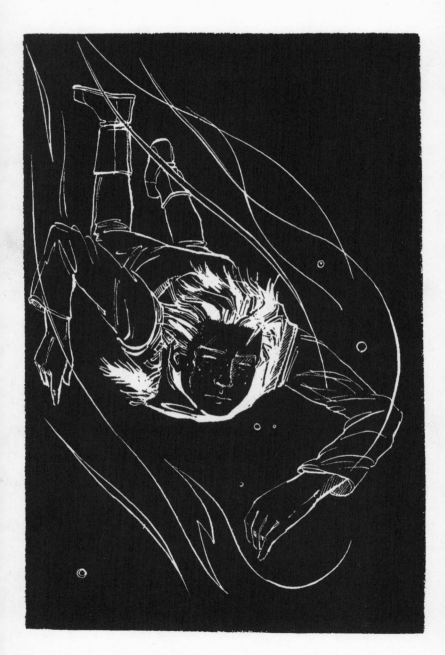

He looked at the thin gap between the water and the rock. How long could they swim under the water and stay alive with no air? Three minutes?

"I'll go first," said Tod.

Once he was under the water, Tod was thrown from one side of the tunnel to the other. He hit the rocky sides again and again. He could not breathe. How far would they have to swim before they came out into the air again?

Chapter 9
Where to Now?

Tod knew he was going to drown.
He thought his lungs were going to burst.
Mum's going to be left alone, he thought
sadly. She would never see him or his dad
again.

Then, just as Tod couldn't hold out any
longer, he was pushed out of the tunnel and
into the air. He could breathe again.

He bumped into his father as he, too, was pushed out of the tunnel.

They were standing with the water up to their waists in a huge cave. A pale light shone from above.

"It's like magic," said Dad.

They pulled themselves out of the water and onto the rocks, lay down on their backs and filled their lungs with fresh air. By the pale light from the crack in the rock above, they could see that their bodies were cut and bleeding. They had been badly knocked about.

"Where are we?" asked Tod.

"This must be the Hollow Hill," Dad told him.

"I thought it was just a story that it was hollow."

"Now we know it's true."

They turned over and drank the water till they had had their fill.

"It's a pity the Bikers found the water," said Tod.

"They'll try and take it all for themselves. We're going to have to find somewhere else to live," said Dad.

Then the sound of an engine filled the cave. They hid behind a rock. Of course the Bikers must know their own city very well, thought Tod.

"Let's get back into the water," he said and was about to move when Dad grabbed him.

"There's no time. Anyway, that's not the sound of a bike. It's more like the noise of your beach buggy."

He was right. The buggy was bumping over the rock floor towards them. It stopped. But who was driving it?

It was Billy, and Tod's mum was sitting beside him.

"What do you think you're doing, Billy? You've nicked my buggy and you've kidnapped my Mum," yelled Tod.

"No, he hasn't done that at all," Mum said. "Billy told me that he knew where you were. But he was scared to go near the mineshaft because of the Bikers. Then he found this cave. But why are you both so wet?"

"It's a long story," Tod told her.

"Let me get at that water," said Billy and he ran over and drank and drank. Tod, Mum and Dad hugged each other.

Then Billy looked up.

"The Bikers are going to kill me for this."

Tod said slowly, "So why don't you come with us? We're moving on."

"That would be great," said Mum. She looked over at Dad and he nodded.

"If that's OK by you, Tod," Dad said.

"It's OK by me." Tod smiled.

He was sure that there were tears in Billy's eyes.

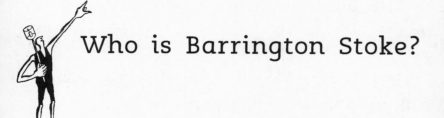

Who is Barrington Stoke?

Barrington Stoke went from place to place with his lamp in his hand. Everywhere he went, he told stories to children. Some were happy, some were sad, some were funny and some were scary.

The children always wanted more. When it got dark, they had to go home to bed. They went to look for Barrington Stoke the next day, but he had gone.

The children never forgot the stories. They told them to each other and to their children and their grandchildren. You see, good stories are magic and they can live forever.

If you loved this story, why don't you read ...

The Hat Trick

by Terry Deary

Is there something you'll remember for as long as you live? When Seaburn football team meet their rivals, Jud has to step in as goalie. Can Jud save the day?

4u2read.ok!

You can order *The Hat Trick* directly from our website at www.barringtonstoke.co.uk